The Curse of PCA

The Curse of PCA

adapted by Jane Mason and Sarah Hines Stephens
based on "The Curse of PCA" written by Dan Schneider

Based on *Zoey 101* created by Dan Schneider

SCHOLASTIC INC.

New York   Toronto   London   Auckland   Sydney
Mexico City   New Delhi   Hong Kong   Buenos Aires

ISBN-10: 0-439-91648-8
ISBN-13: 978-0-439-91648-6

Published by Scholastic Inc.
SCHOLASTIC and associated logos are trademarks and/or registered trademarks of Scholastic Inc.

12 11 10 9 8 7 6 5 4 3 2 1   7 8 9 10 11/0

Printed in the U.S.A.
First printing, September 2007

The Curse of PCA

Cursed

The sun shone down on Pacific Coast Academy. Students in shorts, skirts, and tank tops meandered along the palm-lined paths that ran between the tile-roofed dorms and lecture halls. The cooling ocean breeze was just strong enough to blow everyone's cares away — if they were lucky enough to be outside.

Zoey Brooks and her friends were not that lucky. They were trapped in economics class, where the only wind was the hot air coming from their craggy teacher, Mr. Hodges. He was barking impossible questions at everyone and generally acting as though they were a pack of idiots. He had the entire class fidgeting nervously in their seats, bracing for his next attack.

"Okay, uh. Erhm. Wait . . . uh." Zoey cringed as she

watched her friend Michael struggle to come up with the answer Mr. Hodges was looking for. It was no use. Their economics instructor was so intimidating, it didn't matter if you knew the material or not. When he called on you, you just froze and every thought you ever had went racing out of your head.

"The law of supply . . ." Michael started again.

"Come on!" Hodges roared. "Spit it out!" Mr. Hodges's white hair contrasted sharply with his dark eyebrows, and the way they angled in toward his nose made him look like a furious owl.

"Okay," Michael began again, "the law of supply states price and quality —"

"Quantity!" Mr. Hodges enunciated loudly as if his students were hard of hearing.

"Quantity!" Michael echoed, balling his hand into a tight fist. He'd almost had it. Now if only he could pull it together and answer the question! But before he could even give it another try, Mr. Hodges waved at him dismissively.

"You're hopeless," the instructor growled.

Michael let his fist drop down on his desk, defeated yet again.

Mr. Hodges scanned the faces of the students in

his room from behind his round glasses. His narrowed eyes settled on Zoey. "Brooks!" he barked. "The law of supply states . . ." He rattled off the first part of the sentence and waited for Zoey to finish it.

Zoey started at the sound of her name and flicked her blond hair back over her shoulders. She knew she shouldn't hesitate — Mr. Hodges hated hesitation . . . among other things, like apparently every student in the class. "That the price and quantity supplied are inversely related?" She gave her best educated guess, but her answer still came out like a question.

"No!" Mr. Hodges groaned. Zoey stared glumly at her black-and-royal-blue top, waiting for him to deride her, but Mr. Hodges had already moved on to his next victim. "Dilson!"

The long-haired brunette sitting behind Michael squeaked, a sound she involuntarily resorted to when she was too frightened to scream. The perky pink flower pin on her Route 66 layered shirt seemed to mock her fear. Sitting ramrod straight in her chair, her face was a mask of terror.

"Uh," the teacher groaned and waved his hand, excusing her before he had even asked a question. The petrified girl didn't stand a chance. "Matthews," he said, zeroing in on Chase where he sat on the far side of Zoey.

Chase's brown eyes opened wider, his unruly curls seemed to quiver, and he began to stammer. "That, that, that price and quantity supplied are directly proportional." Chase winced, waiting for the teacher to yell, telling him he was wrong. But he didn't.

"Yes! Hooray!" Mr. Hodges threw his arms up in the air, mocking his class with a sarcastic cheer. "Someone finally said something intelligent," he chided.

Chase breathed a sigh of relief — he'd been called on and not ridiculed for once. Now it was his roommate Logan Reese's turn to sit in the hot seat.

"Reese! The two main branches of economics," the teacher prompted the curly-haired skateboarder, waiting for him to name them.

"Uhhhh . . ." Logan looked baffled and uncomfortable — an unusual look for him. Normally Zoey would have enjoyed seeing Logan squirm, but Mr. Hodges was so relentless, she actually felt a little sorry for him.

"No." Mr. Hodges leaned over his podium. "Not 'Uhhhh.'"

Feeling a little desperate, Zoey put up her hand tentatively. Tension in the classroom was so high it was

giving her a serious headache. "Can I please g⟶
aspirin from the nurse?" she pleaded when the tea⟶
turned her way.

"No. Aspirin is for the weak," Mr. Hodges shot
back, dismissing her immediately.

Zoey glanced at Chase, briefly admiring his
maroon button-down shirt. The color looked good on
him. But fashion aside, was he hearing this? Was this guy
for real? Mr. Hodges had always been strict, but at the
moment he seemed to be going off the deep end.

"Dilson!" Mr. Hodges needled the squeaky brunette for a second time. She sat with her shoulders
hunched, looking like she wished she could become
invisible. No such luck.

"Who was Adam Smith?" Mr. Hodges demanded.

"A political economist and a moral philosopher?"
the girl lisped, her tongue slipping on her retainer.

"Of what country?" Hodges continued.

"Switzerland?" Dilson asked weakly.

"Wrong!"

"Sweden," she offered, cringing.

"Wrong!"

"Scotland?" Her voice was a squeaky whisper.

"Yes," the teacher said, standing up straight.

Dilson looked hopeful . . . for about half a second. "But your shirt is hideous," the teacher announced, obviously needing to find fault with something.

A high-pitched wail erupted out of Dilson's mouth. Leaving her books and bags where they lay, she ran squealing out of the classroom.

"Good riddance," the crotchety teacher shouted after her, leaning across his podium.

Zoey felt a pang of pity and jealousy as the squeal echoed down the hallway. She wanted to run screaming out of class herself. Luckily, at that moment, the bell rang. Everyone leaped to his or her feet, gathering books and bags as quickly as was humanly possible.

"Sit!" Mr. Hodges shouted.

With an audible groan of fear and annoyance at having to stay even a second longer, everyone sank back down in their seats.

"I've decided to give you an exam on Friday," Mr. Hodges said, walking slowly around his podium. The class didn't dare grumble, but the looks on the kids' faces said it all. This was bad news. "You have just two days to become less ignorant," their teacher added tauntingly.

"Can you tell us anything about this exam?" Zoey asked, hoping for some specific topics or chapter numbers, at least.

"Yes, it will be incredibly difficult," Mr. Hodges replied with a smirk.

The class collectively slumped.

"Now . . . " Mr. Hodges sneered, "you may go."

CHAPTER 2

Something to Prove

"Well, it's your own fault for taking his class. Everyone knows Mr. Hodges's reputation," Quinn said matter-of-factly, peering through her square-framed glasses at her friends. Zoey, Logan, Chase, Michael, and Quinn were seated at a large round table with a view over the hills to the ocean. Seagulls wheeled overhead, carefree and beautiful. But they didn't do much for Zoey, Chase, Michael, and Logan, and neither did Quinn's observation. The four economics students were still stunned from their latest torture session — also known as class. Yes, they'd known Hodges was a tough nut going in but . . .

"We didn't know he was the meanest man alive!" Chase threw up his hands in frustration and stared at the hamburger sitting untouched on his tray.

"I hate Hodges," Michael announced, punctuating his statement by crunching loudly on a potato chip.

"You know that he's been at PCA longer than any other teacher?" Quinn raised her eyebrows and flipped one of several slim braids in her long hair over her shoulder.

"He's been *alive* longer than any other teacher," Michael said with disgust. He picked up his soda and tried to wash away the bad taste the announcement of the surprise test had left in his mouth. No luck.

"And this exam? There's no way we're going to be ready," Chase complained.

Quinn looked smug as she sipped her soup. "I warned you guys his class was impossible."

"You just said the work would be *hard*," Zoey pointed out, mildly irritated by her friend's "I told you so" attitude. Zoey wasn't afraid of a little studying. However, she *was* afraid of Mr. Hodges.

"Yeah, you never said Hodges would cause us psychological damage," Chase said, eyeing his tray of food and waiting for his appetite to return. It would really be a shame to waste a perfectly good burger.

"We all know the legend of Charles Galloway," Quinn said a little ominously. Practically every kid in school knew the story of PCA's most famous vanishing student — it was prime PCA lore — and the story alone was enough to keep her out of Hodges's classroom. There was no way her friends could say they hadn't been warned.

"Well, that's true," Michael admitted with a shrug of his broad shoulders.

"I don't." Zoey shook her head. "Who's Charles . . ."

"Galloway," Chase finished.

"He was this kid who went to PCA, like, fifty years ago," Logan explained, sitting back so everyone could see his well-muscled arms. He didn't wear sleeveless tees for nothing, and the black one he currently sported was one of his faves.

"The first year Mr. Hodges started teaching here," Quinn added.

"Yeah, so the story goes that Mr. Hodges gave an exam that was so tough that this Charles kid lost his mind during the test and went insane," Chase explained.

Zoey squinted at her friends, wondering how everyone else knew this story and she didn't. And exactly how crazy could a test make you? "Insane, how?" she asked.

"Fled PCA," Logan said gravely. "Just took off running." Not a bad choice, in a way . . .

"Way up into those mountains." Michael motioned with his hand to the coastal hills behind him. "To that place, uh, what do they call it?"

"Red Stone Gulch," Logan replied.

"So they didn't go get him?" Zoey asked.

Logan shrugged. "They tried."

"They sent out search parties," Michael said, leaning back in his chair and taking another sip of soda.

"But . . . Charles was never found." Logan raised his eyebrows at Zoey, clearly enjoying the spooky tale.

"Aren't those stories just urban legends like Bigfoot, the Triangular Watermelon . . . ?" Chase was not so sure he believed everything he had heard about Charles and Mr. Hodges.

"Well, I think the legend is true," Michael said. "And I bet Charles Galloway is still up there." He glanced back at the hills and tried not to shudder. Suddenly they didn't look so pretty.

"Dude, it's been over fifty years," Chase pointed out. "Nobody can survive in the wilderness that long."

Michael didn't reply, but he looked unconvinced.

Just then Quinn's cell rang. "Quinn," she answered, then paused. "Yeah, on my way," she said to the person on the other end. "Later." She snapped the small silver phone shut and stashed it in her blue-and-white-print backpack.

"Where you headed?" Chase asked.

"Lola put a bowl of apples in the lounge and we're gonna go watch guys eat 'em," Quinn answered with a grin.

"Why?" Michael was baffled, which wasn't all that unusual. He was often perplexed about the things Quinn did. The plans and schemes whirling around in that scientific mind of hers were *waaaaay* beyond him.

"To test their kissability," Quinn answered, like it was the most obvious thing in the world.

Zoey cracked a smile. What would Lola think of next?

"Yes," Michael said, working hard to keep a straight face. "How could I not have known that?"

"Tell me Mr. Hodges's basic theory of the American economy," Chase quizzed Zoey. He was plopped on the floor of her dorm room, sitting in a fuzzy blue beanbag.

Perched on the orange sofa, Zoey flipped frantically through the pages in her spiral notebook. It was hopeless. "When people have money they buy stuff?" she guessed lamely.

Chase made a face. "Yeah, well . . ." He pulled a sheet of paper out of his own notebook. "It's a little more complicated than that." He held up the typed, single-spaced, page-long theory. Actually, try *way* more complicated.

Zoey shut her eyes and Chase noticed that her blue eye shadow matched her electric-blue blouse. She looked awesome, as usual.

Her eyes still closed, Zoey groaned inwardly. She was beginning to feel blue inside, too. "Okay, read it to me and I'll try not to cry," she said dramatically, putting a hand to her head.

"The economy of the United States —"

Chase had only just begun when Logan and Michael burst into the room, excited and out of breath. Michael plunked a book down on the low table between Zoey and Chase and thumped it twice with his index finger, as if that explained everything.

Logan sat down on the bed, then bounced up and pointed at the book excitedly. "Look at that!" he said, puffing out his chest.

"Ha!" Michael exclaimed, triumphant.

Chase eyed his roommates warily. They were acting like they had just won an Oscar, or captured an escaped lion, or solved a major mystery. Just to tease them a little, Chase acted nonchalant, taking his time to pick up the book his roommates were gloating over. "An old PCA yearbook," he said with a shrug. He had a feeling this had something to do with Charles Galloway. . . .

"Over fifty years old," Michael pointed out.

"Check out the page with the pink paper clip," Logan said.

"Pink?" Chase's brows went up, as did Zoey's.

"It was the only color they had at the library," Michael explained quickly, rolling his eyes. Like he would choose pink if he had a choice. "Just look at the page!"

Opening the yearbook, Chase scanned the black-and-white photos until he saw a familiar name. "Charles L. Galloway," he read.

"HA!" Logan and Michael said at the same time and slapped hands.

"Yeah."

"Yeah-he-he-heh."

"So?" Chase said, unclear as to why they were so proud of themselves.

"That just proves he went to school here," Zoey

said, stating the obvious. It was a piece of the puzzle, but not the whole thing.

Michael and Logan opened and closed their mouths like goldfish, both totally speechless.

"It doesn't prove he went nuts and disappeared in the wilderness above PCA," Chase pointed out, eyeing his roommates.

Michael and Logan waved and shrugged and tried to blow it off.

"We know," Michael said, bluffing. He actually hadn't gotten that far. He'd just sort of figured that if Charles Galloway was real, the story was real. But admitting that now would make him look like an idiot. . . .

"Yeah. Yeah," Logan stammered. "We just came by to um . . . to, uh . . ."

Zoey smiled slyly. It was refreshing to see Logan struggle for something to say. The usually ultracool, ultraconfident Logan could be pretty annoying.

"We just came by to, uh —"

"None of your business," Michael blurted. He grabbed the yearbook and hightailed it out of Zoey's room, thunking Chase on the back of the head with the book to hide his embarrassment.

"Yeah!" Logan was hot on Michael's heels, feeling

vaguely uncool. It was a sensation he despised and he was glad to hear the door slam behind them.

When the guys were gone, Chase looked at Zoey, a bit stunned. "He hit me!" he groused, rubbing the back of his head.

An Apple a Day

"Ooh! Two more apple eaters!" Lola pointed to the screen on Quinn's purple laptop. Quinn's tiny computer camera was trained on a large bowl of fruit in the lounge, and from their perch at the high café table, hidden from view, she and Lola could watch boys moving in to enjoy a quick fruit snack.

"You sure you can tell if a guy's a good kisser by the way he eats an apple?" Quinn looked at Lola skeptically. It didn't sound super scientific to her . . . but then she wasn't a boy expert. That was Lola's territory.

"It's a fact," Lola assured her. "Ooh, ooh, *shhh!* Watch." She pointed at the screen, which showed two guys in the lounge who were helping themselves. One of them had blond curly hair, the other had longer brown hair that reached down to his shoulders. Both of them were pretty cute, and both of them picked up juicy red apples and took big bites.

"Oh, yeah, I think that guy with the longer hair is from Texas," Quinn said. She had seen him around campus a few times.

"Uh-huh. The other one's Australian." Lola pointed at the blond, practically squealing. An Australian sweetie would have its benefits. "I love accents! Zoom in tighter."

Quinn pushed a few buttons while the guys unknowingly munched away.

"Okay, now *he* is a good kisser." Lola nodded, watching the way one of the guys bit into the apple.

"Who? Texas?"

"No, the Australian short-hair," Lola said, almost laughing. It sounded like she was talking about a dog!

Quinn watched the Australian take a thoughtful-looking bite. "Oh, yeah," she agreed, though she wasn't entirely sure exactly what she was looking for — she didn't know that much about boys, but apples were one of her favorite fruits . . . along with bananas.

And speaking of boys . . . she could not stop thinking about the boy who went crazy right there at PCA. "Hey, you've heard the story about Charles Galloway, right?" she asked Lola, peering over the top of her glasses. Just the sound of his name was intriguing. He kind of sounded like a famous actor.

"That PCA kid who, like, freaked out about fifty years ago?" Lola asked. She pushed a few more keys on the computer keyboard and zoomed in even tighter on the apple eaters.

"Yeah," Quinn confirmed. That was the guy. "Wouldn't it be great if we could prove whether the legend is true or not?" Quinn loved a good mystery almost as much as she loved science.

"How could we prove it?" Lola wondered aloud. She turned away from the screen. Her big pink shell earrings — the ones that perfectly matched the ribbon ties on her printed tank top — swung slightly, as she gave Quinn her undivided attention.

"Well, if he really did live in the wilderness above PCA for a bunch of years, there'd have to be some sign of him, right?" Quinn said logically.

Lola furrowed her brow. "Oh, you mean up at that place . . ." She snapped her fingers trying to come up with the name of the spot where Charles Galloway had disappeared.

"Red Stone Gulch," Quinn said excitedly, clasping her hands and jangling her bright red bracelets.

"Yeah, I thought it was impossible to get up there without, like, a helicopter." Lola was so busy talking, she didn't notice the cute guy in the PCA T-shirt walking up behind her until he spoke.

"Not impossible," he interjected, flashing Lola and Quinn a winning smile.

Lola flashed her own killer smile right back. "Hi!" she said admiringly. The guy was tall, had an adorable part-rocker/part-surfer haircut, and wore a cool collection of leather necklaces.

Quinn scowled. Who was this guy, and how did he get in their conversation? "Hello," she said cautiously.

"You guys wanna hike up to Red Stone Gulch?" the guy asked, crossing his tanned arms over his chest and grinning confidently.

Lola flashed Quinn a hopeful look.

"'Cause I could take you there," the guy offered.

"We don't even know you," Quinn balked. Was he crazy? Couldn't he see he was interrupting?

"Yes, please take us there!" Lola said enthusiastically, drowning Quinn out. This would be the perfect opportunity to hike up to Red Stone Gulch with the cutest guide on campus!

"Can we at least ask the boy his name?" Quinn looked at Lola like she was out of her head. She knew her friend was boy-crazy, but she didn't have to be *crazy*-crazy!

"I'm Lafe," Lafe said with a chuckle.

"Lola." Lola beamed back at him.

"Quinn," Quinn said with a shrug. She clearly couldn't stop Lola from going along with this foolish plan, so she may as well go along to watch out for her friend, and maybe even find out if the Charles Galloway rumor was true.

"Uh, can we bring some friends?" Lola asked quickly. Zoey would not want to miss this!

"The more the hikier," Lafe said, forcing a laugh.

Lola giggled, even though that was one of the worst jokes she had heard all year. Lafe was just so cute!

Quinn gave her friend a hard look. Did Lola honestly think that was funny? She really had lost it!

Lola raised her eyebrows back at Quinn, giving her a look that said, "Don't mess this up for me." She seriously hoped Quinn would get her meaning, and get it fast!

Who Brought the Mustard?

"Please! Please, don't make me do this!" Chase begged his two best friends and roommates to let go of his arms. First of all, it was a little embarrassing to be dragged across campus. And second, he didn't want any part of Red Stone Gulch or Charles Galloway!

"Come on," Michael coaxed, adjusting his backpack and his walking stick in his free hand. "Where's your sense of adventure?"

"Our economics test is going to be an adventure, okay? A very bad adventure ... that we should be studying for!" Chase argued.

"*After* we hike up to Red Stone Gulch," Logan insisted. He hadn't been able to stop thinking about Charles Galloway since his name came up at lunch yesterday. If Logan could prove Galloway was real, he'd be famous, not to mention that he might be able to get his dad to make a movie about him!

"There's nothing up there," Chase insisted, pulling his arms free. The dudes were rumpling his blue plaid button-down.

"Well," Michael said, releasing Chase, "when you prove that, you can say 'I told you so.'"

Chase looked at his roommates. They were serious about this, and they both wanted him to come along. It was two against one. "Who is this Lafe guy, anyway?" he asked, annoyed.

"He's a senior," Logan told him.

Chase rolled his eyes.

"And Lola says he can lead us up there, no problem," Michael assured them. "And that he's super cute."

Chase and Logan turned to look at Michael, who was holding his hands up in surrender and wishing he could rewind his mouth. "Her words," he said defensively as Chase and Logan headed off to their designated meeting point. He was just repeating what Lola said.

A few minutes later, Chase, Logan, and Michael were staring skeptically at their "guide" while they waited for the girls. He looked like a regular enough dude, but hiking up to Red Stone Gulch was not going to be a picnic — otherwise the legend of Charles Galloway would have been proven by now!

"So, how'd your parents come up with the name Lafe?" Logan asked, trying to make conversation. He hoped the girls would show up soon. He was ready to get going on this hike — and if they didn't head out soon, Chase might try to back out again.

"It's a combination of 'life' and 'hope,'" Lafe explained, gesturing with his walking stick.

"Then shouldn't you be 'Lofe?'" Chase asked, squinting in the bright sunlight and questioning his decision to come along.

"Well, yeah, but Lofe would sound dumb," Lafe said with an awkward laugh.

"Yeah." *Exactly.* Chase and the other guys all chuckled. Chase couldn't help himself but this guy was obviously not the brightest crayon in the box. "Unlike 'Lafe,' which sounds so intell —"

"Look!" Michael interrupted Chase before he got his foot stuck all the way in his mouth. Why would you want to make fun of the guy who was about to be responsible for your safety? "Here come the girls."

Zoey, Lola, and Quinn walked up dressed in tank tops and comfy pants. They had backpacks on and sweatshirts tied around their waists. They looked impressively ready to go.

"Hey, guys!" they greeted the boys.

"Hello, girls," Michael shot back.

They were all there. Finally. Chase just wanted to get this over with so he could finish studying for his econ exam.

"Okay." Lafe brought his hands together like he was calling a meeting to order. "We got us a nice day for a hike. Oh, and since cell phones won't work up in the mountains, I brought us some walkies." He pulled a walkie-talkie out of his back pocket and tossed it to Chase. "One for you. And one for you." He handed another one to Quinn.

"Thank you." Quinn took it and looked it over, smiling. She loved technology, and it was smart of Lafe to think about communication. Maybe he really could get them up to Red Stone Gulch.

"And, uh, let's see, everybody got some water?" Lafe asked.

The gang all patted their water bottles.

"Yup."

"Yeah."

"Water, right here!"

"Sunblock?" Lafe asked next.

"Mmm-hmm."

"Yep."

"Always."

So far everybody had what they needed, so Lafe continued with his checklist. It was essential to be prepared. "Mustard?" he asked.

The group of friends went silent and gave Lafe a collective look of disbelief. Did he actually say *mustard?*

Lafe's expression was serious — for a second. Then he cracked up. "Hey, I'm just yanking your tongues a little bit."

Lola faked a laugh at the odd joke. Zoey looked at Quinn out of the corners of her eyes, wondering if this guy could possibly be as dim as he seemed. Quinn just blinked.

"Mustard?" Lafe repeated, still laughing along with Lola. Then his expression got serious. "I got plenty for all of us," he said. He reached into one of the deep pockets of his brown cargo pants, pulled out a large yellow tube, and showed it to the crew before stashing it back in the pocket and giving it a pat.

Whoa. Zoey rolled her eyes. He wasn't kidding! Suddenly Michael and Logan did not look so confident about their "guide."

"Okay, let's roll!" Lafe said enthusiastically as he led the way off campus, putting his walking stick firmly on the ground with each step.

"Yeah."

"Let's roll," Michael said a little doubtfully.

Everyone began to follow Lafe. Chase waited for Zoey to catch up. "Why would we want mustard on a —"

"I don't know," Zoey answered before Chase could finish the question. In fact, she didn't know how she got talked into going on this hike in the first place. And she was not ready to discuss it.

Unfortunately the bad omens continued. "Okay, wait, wait. Hold off!" They had only been walking a little while — they were still on the paved road behind PCA — when Zoey stopped the hikers.

"What's the problem?" Logan asked.

"Will you just look at that sign?" Zoey pointed at a yellow triangular caution sign by the side of the road. It pictured a coiled rattlesnake and in large black type read: CAUTION SNAKES.

"I-I-I don't like snakes," Michael stammered, his eyes wide. He didn't think of himself as a wimp or anything, but snakes . . . "I don't even like worms, their smaller, weaker cousins," he finished weakly.

"Yeah, me either," Chase agreed with a shudder.

Quinn laughed and waved a hand at the guys, as if she could brush away their fears. "Relax," she said, putting her hands on her hips. "If we're bothered by a dangerous snake, I can protect us," she bragged.

"How?" Michael asked, his curiosity momentarily roused. Within a single second he regretted asking, however.

Quinn grinned, took Michael by the elbow, and dragged him away from the group. "What? Wait. Why me?" Michael protested. "You got five other friends over there!" Why was he always Quinn's guinea pig?

The five friends watched from a safe distance, glad they had not been chosen to be part of Quinn's demonstration, while she pulled Michael several yards away. Stopping, she took a gadget off of the tool belt she had slung around her hips and opened it.

"What are you going to do?" Michael asked nervously. Quinn's inventions usually had a huge impact.

"Shhh!" Quinn shushed him. She opened the small case and removed a slim silver tool — it looked like a metal straw. Slowly she put it to her lips, took aim at a cactus, and blew.

The sound of detonating explosives thundered through the air and the cactus burst into flames. When the fireball cleared, the entire desert plant had vanished, leaving only a patch of scorched earth.

The hikers put up their hands to protect themselves from the rocks and dirt that showered down on them in the aftermath.

"Oh, yeah!" Quinn grinned triumphantly at the spot where the cactus had been. Her execution was flawless, as usual.

Michael could not believe his eyes. "That'd shake up a snake," he said, his voice cracking. He just hoped Quinn's aim wasn't off.

"Ha," Quinn gloated. Of course it would. Another of her inventions, perfected!

"Onward and upward!" Lafe said to the hikers, and began hoofing up the mountain once more. It was time to get this mustard show on the road!

The group panted in the heat as dust swirled around their feet. They had been hiking for what felt like forever, and Red Stone Gulch was nowhere in sight.

"Whoa! Let's hold up for a sec," Lafe called out. Holding his yellow compass in his hand, he stepped off the trail to study it.

Zoey looked at Chase. Chase looked at Zoey. They

both knew they were thinking the same thing. What did they need to hold on for? They should have been there by now.

"Well?" Chase asked, holding up his arms and waiting for Lafe's report.

"Where's Red Stone Gulch?" Zoey asked, getting to the point. She didn't have Chase's patience.

"Yeah, we've been hiking for three hours," Chase added, relieved that Zoey had said what he was thinking. Chase could have used those three hours to study instead of following their bonehead guide around the hot California hills.

"Lafe knows what he's doing!" Lola told her friends defensively, before turning to Lafe. "You know what you're doing, right?" she asked, doing her best to ignore the nagging feeling she had in her gut.

"Oh, yeah," Lafe said a little awkwardly. "I'm just a little confused by my compass." He stared at the small direction-giving device in his hand, then gave it a shake.

Chase scrambled up the trail to take a look. Tired of wasting time, he took the compass right out of Lafe's hand and stared at the needle behind the glass. It was spinning wildly, swinging in all directions.

"That's weird," Chase muttered.

Logan rolled his eyes impatiently. How hard could this be? "Which way's north?" he demanded.

"Well, according to this compass, north is that way, that way, that way, this way, and apparently just to the left of my bladder," Chase said, pointing in nearly every direction.

Zoey groaned out loud. She was *never* going to get any study time in at this rate! None of the other hikers looked too happy about the situation, either. "All right, I have to study for my test, so can we please go back to PCA, right now?" Zoey pleaded.

"Well, fair enough," Lafe said with a chuckle. Shrugging his broad shoulders, he looked around for a moment before pointing in the general direction they'd come from. "Okay, back to PCA," he said. But he didn't move. Instead he started to ramble. "Pacific Coast Academy. Ocean views." He sounded more like a brochure advertising the school than a hiking guide.

"You don't know the way back, do you?" Zoey asked, putting a hand on her hip.

"No, I do not." Lafe laughed nervously. "Although I do have some mustard." He pulled out his big yellow tube.

Logan and Zoey looked at each other. Michael slapped the mustard out of Lafe's grasp. Chase hid his face in his hand. They were somewhere in the foothills of California with a bottle of mustard, a broken compass, and no idea how to get back to PCA.

5
Lost

The sun was getting lower in the sky. The level of water in the hikers' water bottles was getting lower as well. Things were not looking good.

Sitting in the red dirt with her legs folded, Zoey scowled at Lafe as he dug into the dry soil. He got them into this mess, shouldn't he at least be trying to get them out of it? "Okay, how is scooping up dirt going to get us down this mountain and back to PCA?" she asked, giving their guide a hard look.

"By throwing dirt dust in the air I can tell which way the wind is blowing and that will help me get a directional bearing back to PCA." Lafe *sounded* like an expert, but when he gave a little triumphant cheer and tossed the dirt upward, it all rained back down on his head and face, making him *look* like a chump. "Oh, huh-huh." He tried to laugh while spitting out dust.

"So, the way back to PCA is through Lafe's face," Michael said, deadpan. He was losing his sense of humor fast.

Lafe grabbed his walking stick and put his sunglasses back on. He peered up in the sky where a faint quacking could be heard. "Hey, Mexican ducks!" he said excitedly.

"Who cares?" Logan muttered. They were totally lost and Lafe was all excited about some stupid birds? Uh, hello, this wasn't exactly a good time for bird-watching!

"Well, they're creatures of nature," Lafe said. "They can show us the way."

"What?" Michael was just about done listening to Mustard Boy.

"They're ducks," Logan said slowly, so Lafe could keep up. Ducks had tiny brains, quacked, and did not attend Pacific Coast Academy. How could they possibly show them the way back?

"Wait! Wait up!" Lafe called to his flying friends. When they did not respond, he tried again in Spanish. *"Esperame. Esperame."*

Zoey rolled her eyes. Lola laughed uncomfortably. "Okay," she admitted. "He's not a very good guide." She hoped her friends would forgive her.

"Just go after him so he doesn't get more lost," Chase said with a sigh.

"Okay." Lola started to go.

"Oh, wait. Take a walkie." Chase handed over his walkie-talkie.

"Thanks." Lola accepted it gratefully, then took off at a run to catch Lafe and the ducks. "Lafe! Wait!" she called as he disappeared behind a manzanita tree.

As Chase watched Lola disappear in the scrub brush, he wondered if she could actually improve Lafe's navigational skills. He doubted it. Turning back to his friends, he stared. "Uh-oh. Quinn has something weird attached to her face."

Logan, Michael, and Zoey looked up at Quinn.

"They're Quinnoculars," Quinn said proudly, lowering the huge, bizarre-looking yellow opticals. "Five lenses, see?" She showed everyone the multiple tubes of lenses on her handy gadget.

"Why five?" Michael asked. As far as he was concerned, one good set of lenses was plenty.

"More powerful, better optical clarity, night vision, *and* they even let you see through some things in bright sunlight," Quinn explained.

"You can't see *through* things," Chase scoffed.

That required X-ray vision. No way had Quinn invented her own X-ray vision binoculars.

Zoey watched as Quinn leveled her Quinnoculars at Chase.

The invention beeped softly as Quinn pushed a series of lighted buttons on the side. "Boxer briefs," she announced, lowering the glasses and staring at Chase with a smirk on her face.

Chase's jaw dropped and he turned away, blushing and feeling more than a little exposed.

Meanwhile, Lafe was still running after the ducks. "Ducks, hey! *¡Ayudame! ¡Estoy perdido! ¡Yo quiero volar como tu!*"

"Lafe! Hey!" Lola panted, finally catching up to him on a wide dirt trail under a scrawny tree.

"The ducks flew away," Lafe said sadly, clearly disappointed.

"Yes," Lola said with a nod. She actually felt a little sorry for him. "That's what ducks do."

"Oh."

The dude sounded pretty bummed, and Lola decided now was not the time to tell him what an idiot he was for getting them all lost.

"Lola, did you find Lafe?" The walkie on Lola's belt crackled and Zoey's voice came through the speaker.

"Yeah," Lola reported, brushing some dust off her blue-and-red long tank. "I got him. We'll circle around and meet you guys in about fifteen."

"All right," Zoey confirmed.

With a sigh, Lola turned to Lafe. He looked like he had something on his mind. Something besides Spanish-speaking ducks.

"Um, I have a confession to make," he said sheepishly. "I'm not really that good a hiking guide."

"Noooo." Lola feigned shock and surprise, calling upon her acting skills. This was news?

"Nah, it's true," Lafe said, nodding earnestly. It was clear that he had completely missed the sarcasm in Lola's voice.

"Then why did you say you could lead us to Red Stone Gulch?" Lola asked, getting exasperated.

"Well . . ." Lafe nervously looked down at his hiking boots. His hair hung forward, shading his big brown eyes, and he scuffed his toes in the dust. "I don't know, I guess I kind of wanted to hang out with you," he confessed. He looked back up into Lola's face. "Is that bad?"

Lola felt her anger start to melt. The puppy-dog

look always got her. Lafe was awfully cute. And he had done all this for her! But now she and her friends were lost in the hills, hours away from school, with no idea how to get back . . . all because Lafe had lied. She had to be honest. "It's not good, Lafe," she told him firmly.

"Oh, I knew it!" Lafe threw back his head like he had been hit. "I'm unappealing!"

"No," Lola told him. That wasn't actually it at all. Lack of appeal was *not* Lafe's problem. Still, there was a problem, and she had to tell him. "But you lied and now you got us all lost."

"Hey, lost just means you found something you weren't looking for," Lafe said, trying to look on the bright side.

Lola chose to ignore the lame touchy-feely comment. "Let's just get back to the others, okay?"

"Sure," Lafe agreed. "I'll lead the way."

Lola turned to follow. "Log," she called out, warning her fearless leader. Too late. Lafe fell right over the large limb blocking the path.

Jumping to his feet, Lafe turned back toward Lola and tried to look cool. "Careful, there's a log there," he cautioned her.

"Thanks," Lola replied, gingerly stepping over the log with a smirk.

From high atop Michael's shoulders, Quinn had a pretty good view. But even with the help of her amazing Quinnoculars, she could not spot Red Stone Gulch.

"Can you see anything?" Zoey asked, looking up at the girl balanced on Michael, who was balanced on a good-sized rock.

"No," Quinn sighed. "I'll boost the zoom on my Quinnoculars." She pushed a button and the handy optical device beeped and whirred as it zoomed in on the arid hill in the distance.

Zoey wondered why Quinn was looking up the hill and not down toward campus. "I thought we decided to forget Red Stone Gulch and find our way back to PCA so we can study for our test," she told her friends impatiently. She looked at Chase with pleading eyes. He was with her on this, right?

"Yeah, it's going to be dark in a couple of hours, anyway," Chase agreed. He was not too psyched about the idea of being stuck here at night.

"You just want to leave because you know we're going to find out the legend of Charles Galloway is true," Michael accused, swaying a little under Quinn's weight. He'd been holding her for what seemed like forever.

"Yeah," Logan agreed, giving Chase a "what are you, chicken?" look.

Chase's and Zoey's shoulders slumped in unison. If they wanted to leave now, they would be in for a fight. The guys were dead set on solving their little mystery.

"AAAAAAH!" Suddenly Quinn screamed, startling all of them.

"Whoa!" Michael almost fell.

"Whoa!" Logan almost got smashed.

"I think I see Red Stone Gulch!" Quinn squealed, resettling the binoculars in front of her eyes for another look.

"Ha-ha-ha-ha-ha!" Michael laughed, swaggering as best he could while holding Quinn. They were getting closer and closer to proving the myth of Charles L. Galloway was no myth after all!

Final Resting Place

"Lafe, maybe you should let me lead the way?" Lola suggested . . . again. It seemed like they should have gotten back to the others a while ago.

"I'm telling you we're almost — oh." Lafe stopped in his tracks and stared at the path.

Lola lifted her sunglasses. Right in front of them was the very same log Lafe had tripped over when they'd started off to find the rest of the group. "Isn't this where we were fifteen minutes ago?" she asked, feeling instantly annoyed and planting her hands on her hips.

"Uh, yeah!" Lafe replied with his signature goofy laugh.

Lola shot him a look.

"You're irritated with me," Lafe guessed.

"Kinda," Lola said, unsmiling. That was an understatement.

Lafe nervously tapped his walking stick on the ground and looked away. "I knew it."

Meanwhile, Chase, Zoey, Logan, Michael, and Quinn had made it to Red Stone Gulch. Chase jumped off the last small ledge into the wide ravine behind his friends, surprised to discover that he was kind of excited to be here.

"Here we are!" Quinn said with a celebratory grin.

"See? We made it." Michael was smiling widely, too. He just knew they could find Red Stone Gulch without a helicopter, and they had. All they had was one another, Quinn's Quinnoculars, and the worst hiking guide at PCA! "Red Stone Gulch!"

"Ha!" Logan said in Chase and Zoey's direction. They were about to prove everything, he could feel it.

"Why are you 'ha-ing'?" Zoey asked, annoyed. She was hot, thirsty, tired . . . and she had barely even started to study for her econ exam.

"We haven't proved that Charles Galloway was ever here," Chase pointed out, slipping off his pack. His shoulders were aching and it was seriously hot.

"Just wait!" Logan said, pointing his finger at his friends like he was about to teach them a lesson.

"We're gonna find evidence," Michael added, nodding. He threw his arm over Logan's shoulder — they were a team on this, and Chase and Zoey were the naysayers.

"Yup!" Quinn agreed, unloading a bunch of odd-looking gear from her pack. "I brought a portable metal detector."

"Of course you did." Chase did not know why he was surprised. Nothing Quinn did should surprise him anymore.

Quinn quickly assembled her equipment. "It also detects crabs, medical waste, and various types of animal urine," she explained as the device buzzed into action.

"Well, now I know what to buy Grandma for Christmas," Zoey said sarcastically, wondering who would want to detect crabs . . . or medical waste . . . or animal urine . . . besides Quinn, of course. Zoey watched glumly as Quinn began beeping and scanning the gulch. It was at least thirty feet across! This was going to take the rest of the day.

On another part of the hill, Lola was still annoyed. Really annoyed. "I can't believe you got yourself, me, and five other people lost in the wilderness just because you wanted to hang out with me," she said, not bothering to hide any of her frustration.

"You think I'm silly," Lafe said sheepishly.

"No, Lafe, SpongeBob's friend Patrick is silly. I think you're a weirdo!" Lola exclaimed.

"Okay, so, I'm a little bit out there," Lafe admitted in a goofy voice.

"If by 'out there' you mean crazy? Yeah, you're out there," Lola agreed.

"Ah, I am but mad north, northwest. When the wind is southerly I know a hawk from a handsaw."

Lola stopped walking. She could not believe her ears! "That's from *Hamlet*," she said, smiling. "That's, like, my second-favorite play."

Lafe leaped lightly across a small gulley and reached back to give Lola a hand. "What's your fave?" he asked with a charming smile.

"*The Importance of Being Earnest*," Lola answered quickly.

"Oh, yeah, I know it. Um, let's see." Lafe took a second and then began reciting lines in an English accent. "My dear sir, the way you flirt with Gwendolyn is perfectly disrespectful."

Lola joined in.

44

"It's almost as bad as the way Gwendolyn flirts with you!" they said in unison.

"Excellent," Lafe complimented Lola. "So, you're an actress."

"Totally." Lola nodded. Her annoyance was fading, and she found it really hard not to smile. Lafe might be out there, but he had great taste in plays!

"Nice. So, are you a hungry actress?" Lafe asked.

"Starved," Lola admitted.

"All right." Lafe sat down and opened his pack. "Tangerine for you," he said, passing her the fruit. "Apple for me."

Lola's mind spun. She heard Quinn's voice in her head as she watched Lafe dig into his snack. *"Are you sure you can tell if a guy's a good kisser by the way he eats an apple?"* she had asked. *"It's a fact,"* Lola had answered. She watched Lafe closely as Lafe ate his apple. It all looked promising. And now the time had come to test her theory. . . .

Lafe looked up from his fruit and caught the twinkle in Lola's eye. "What?" he asked.

Lola answered by leaning in for a kiss.

"Sweet," Lafe said when she pulled away, then quickly kissed her again.

*   *   *

Meanwhile, Logan and Michael were checking under tumbleweeds and kicking up dust in search of a sign of Charles Galloway. Several feet away, Quinn scanned the gulch with her metal detector. A few boarded-up entrances to an old mine or shelter of some kind were built into the hill. Chase and Zoey did their best to see inside, but almost all of the openings were sealed up tight. Only one small chamber was open and it was completely deserted.

"You guys find anything?" Zoey called out to the others as she and Chase emerged from the hollow.

"Nope, not yet," Logan answered.

"Anything in there?" Michael asked.

"Nope." Zoey shook her head.

"Empty," Chase answered.

Suddenly Quinn's metal detector started going crazy. "Hey, hey, I found something!" she called excitedly.

Zoey and the others rushed over to Quinn, hoping it wasn't animal urine, or worse, that had set the machine off.

Michael, Quinn, and Logan dropped to their knees and began digging in the red dusty dirt. About five inches down, Quinn's hand closed around something and she pulled it up. It only took a second to see that it was a chain of some sort, with a pair of metal tags, kind of like dog tags, hanging from it.

"What is it?" Zoey asked.

"It looks like an old PCA necklace." Michael took the chain from Quinn and tried to scrub the dirt off the tags with his thumb. "Gimme some water."

Logan handed over his near-empty bottle of water and Michael poured a few precious drops over the dusty tags. "I think there's a name on the back, but I can't make the letters out."

"I bet I can read it." Quinn walked back to where her backpack was lying on the ground, fifteen feet away. She grabbed her Quinnoculars and put them to her face. "Hold it up," she called back to Michael. "Steady. Keep it really still." She set the Quinnoculars to see through grime, enhanced the image, and read: "Charles . . . L. . . . Galloway!"

"Yes!"

"Yes!"

Logan and Michael began cheering, pumping fists, shaking hands, and slapping five like they had just won the Superbowl.

"Charles L. Galloway!" Michael sang at Chase, mocking him.

"So it's true," Zoey said, feeling unimpressed. She

didn't really care if the legend was true — she just wanted to get back to PCA, eat something, take a shower, and study for her exam!

"I guess this means we're standing right where he . . . you know . . ." Logan paused, feeling kind of weird. "Died," he finished uncomfortably.

"Yeah."

"Oh."

"Um, probably right around here."

Everyone took a few steps back, creeped out by the notion that they might be standing on some poor teenager's unmarked grave.

"Okay, you guys were right, the legend is true." Zoey had to admit the necklace proved it. "Now put it back and let's get out of here."

"Put it back?" Logan scoffed, holding the necklace tightly in his fist. "Are you crazy?" They had been hiking around for hours trying to get this thing and Zoey wanted him to put it back? No way.

"It's not ours to take," Chase pointed out. It belonged to some dead guy!

"Dude, this necklace is, like, our proof," Logan argued. "We'll be famous at PCA as the people who proved the legend of Charles Galloway! And I own the movie rights," he added, pointing at each of them.

"You don't mess with a man's eternal resting place," Michael said gravely. He felt kinda bad for going against Logan, but taking the necklace just didn't seem right.

"I agree," Quinn said.

"We leave it where we found it," Zoey told Logan. Her voice was calm. She meant it.

"You guys!" Logan protested. Nobody would ever believe that they'd found it!

"We leave it where we found it," Chase repeated evenly. They were all in agreement — all of them except Logan.

"Okay, I'll put it back," Logan moped.

"And don't even think about trying to steal it!" Chase said, pointing at his friend. He knew that Logan could not be trusted. "'Cause we're going to frisk you."

Logan didn't look scared.

"Everywhere," Chase added.

"I'm not going to steal it," Logan said, acting offended. Chase walked away and Logan bent down over the hole where they'd found the chain. Glancing back at the others, he pushed the necklace into the dirt, then pulled it back out and hid it in his palm.

"Hey," Zoey called to Logan from a few feet away. "When you're done, bring me my backpack, okay?"

"Sure," Logan answered. He patted the ground a few times to make it look like he was really burying the tags, then walked over to Zoey's pack and slipped the necklace inside one of the small outer pockets.

"Thanks," Zoey said when Logan handed her the pack a few seconds later. She took a walkie off of the side and called the other two hikers. "Lola? Lola? Are you there?"

"Hey, Zoey, it's me," Lola answered quickly.

"We found Charles Galloway's dog tags," Zoey reported.

"No way!"

"Yep, the legend is true," Zoey confirmed.

"That's so cool," Lola said excitedly.

Above them the sky rumbled.

"Was that thunder?" Lola's voice crackled through the walkie-talkie.

Zoey furrowed her brow. Whatever it was, it hadn't sounded good.

"Yeah." Chase took the walkie-talkie out of Zoey's hand and spoke into it. "Don't try and find us, just head back to PCA."

"How?" Lola asked. "We don't know where we are."

"Well, we went *up* to get here. Just go down," Chase instructed. "We'll meet you at the lounge."

"Okay, we'll try." Lola turned back to Lafe. He was holding up a yellow plastic bottle.

"Mustard?" he offered.

"I'm good," Lola said with a sigh. The guy was definitely a little quirky . . . and sweet. She took one more look at Lafe before heading down the hill. Good-looking? Definitely. Good actor? Maybe. Good leader? No way. She was going to have to get them back herself.

CHAPTER 7
Struck Down

Overhead, the sound of thunder grew louder. The sky grew darker with surprising speed and a gusty wind began to blow, stirring up dust and making it hard for Zoey and her friends to see. Zoey's hair whipped her face.

"Wow!" Michael shouted between gusts. "That storm is coming in pretty fast." Only moments before it had been a hot, calm, clear afternoon.

"Yeah," Logan agreed, looking around nervously. "Let's get out of here."

"Let's go." Together the five kids headed up the wall of Red Stone Gulch, leaving Charles Galloway's grave behind.

Lightning crackled, making the hikers jump. Though it was hard to see the trail, they began to run. Branches scraped against their arms and legs.

Suddenly there was a horrible flash and the loudest rumble of thunder Zoey had ever heard echoed through the hills. Somebody screamed. Before Zoey knew it, they were all screaming — Michael loudest of all.

The group stumbled into a clearing and paused to catch their breath.

"I've never seen a storm come in this fast!" Quinn said, gasping. "The barometric conditions must be —"

At that moment a bolt of lightning touched the ground in the middle of the clearing, blowing everyone off their feet.

"That lightning almost hit us!" Logan yelled.

"I don't like lightning!" Michael shouted. His voice was filled with panic. "I don't like it at all!"

"It's just weather," Quinn shouted back, trying to calm him down.

The wind kept blowing in all directions, howling and kicking up more dust. Zoey looked at Chase. Then she heard something else. A new sound . . . a deep, groaning moan! As Chase and Zoey watched, a strange green fog began to form over the bush behind Quinn, Michael, and Logan.

"What is that?" Chase demanded, pointing at the strange apparition. "*Green* weather?"

The others turned to see what Chase was pointing

at. The green mist swirled, becoming a larger and larger cloud as it made its way closer. The fog was lit from behind by a fork of lightning, but even after the lightning faded, the green mist appeared to glow on its own.

"Would somebody please tell me what that is?" Zoey pleaded, unable to take her eyes off of it.

For once Quinn did not have an answer. "I don't know!" she screamed, throwing up her hands.

Lightning struck the ground again, dangerously close to Logan's foot. Everyone screamed.

"What do we do?" Logan shouted.

Chase was on his feet with the answer. "Run!" he shouted. "Run!"

He didn't have to say it twice. Quinn scrambled down the mountain, screaming all the way. Chase and Michael were right behind her. At a fork in the path, Quinn went left, and the boys followed. But the groaning was coming closer!

Blinded by a flash of lightning, Zoey missed the path her friends had taken.

Chase ran as fast as he could down the darkened trail behind Michael. He could hear his roommate bellowing. And behind him . . . nothing but howling wind.

"Zoey?" Chase turned. She was right there a minute ago, but now he couldn't see her. "Zoey?" he called, stopping to listen. Nothing. He had to go back. Turning, he ran back up the trail, toward the awful groaning whatever-it-was. "Where'd you go?" Chase screamed into the storm.

"Hey!" Zoey called out for her friends to slow down — she had no idea they were no longer ahead of her. They seemed to have disappeared! Moving fast, she pushed past a shrub and stepped out into nothingness. The ground fell away and Zoey fell with it. She came down hard on her left ankle, collapsing onto the packed soil. The walkie-talkie went flying and the wind swept away her scream.

Struggling to get to her feet, Zoey crumpled back to the ground. Searing pain shot through her ankle. She'd twisted it badly. She couldn't walk!

"Chase!" Zoey screamed, holding her throbbing leg. "Chase!" she yelled again. Thunder rumbled, drowning her out. She tried again to walk, but it was too painful. She was stranded.

CHAPTER 8

The Chase

The green fog kept getting bigger and creepier as it rolled down the mountainside behind Zoey. It was heading straight down the path where she was stranded. Shuddering, she tried not to look, but she knew that the gusting, moaning wind was bringing it closer and closer.

She had to get out of there! Lurching to her feet, she tried to continue down the mountain. But her ankle buckled painfully and she fell back to the ground.

"Chase!" she called into the stormy sky. "Chase!" Where was he?

Don't panic, Zoey told herself, fully aware that it was a little late to be giving herself that advice. Like it or not, at this point, alone, hurt, and lost, she was fully freaked.

Inching forward on her hands and knees, she tried to keep going. But her progress was slow and the creepy fog was getting closer by the second!

"Chaaaaase!" she screamed into the wind yet again.

Then suddenly something grabbed her by the arm! Chase! Zoey had never been so happy to see anyone in her life.

"Come on, let's go," Chase said, frantically eyeing the approaching mass of green.

"I can't — I hurt my ankle," Zoey replied. The wind was gusting so hard, it was difficult to hear or see clearly, let alone think. How were they going to get off the mountain?

Chase didn't hesitate. Reaching forward, he picked Zoey up in his arms and carried her down the trail as fast as he could.

Not far in front of them, Quinn, Logan, and Michael were beating it to the PCA student lounge — screaming all the way. Closer to the school, the weather was much calmer, and the sound of their shouting echoed across campus.

When they burst into the lounge, Lola and Lafe were already there, cuddling on the couch.

"Ahhhhhh!" Michael shrieked as he flew through the doors.

"What?" Lola asked calmly.

"What?" Quinn echoed, sounding completely freaked out. Her braids were a mess and her jacket was askew around her shoulders.

"What?" Michael's heart thudded frantically in his chest.

"Why are you guys freaking out?" Lola asked.

"Because it's appropriate to freak out when you've been attacked and chased down a mountain by a . . . a . . ." Michael had no idea what that thing was . . . or at least, he didn't want to admit it. "By a you-know-what!"

Lafe shrugged. "It was just a storm."

Quinn eyed their supposed hiking guide with fury, and before she knew it she was grabbing him by the shoulders and shaking him with all her might. "Just a storm!" she shrieked. "Just a storm?!"

"Quinn!" Lola struggled to push her friend off of her new sweetie just as Logan practically fell into the room and onto a chair, gasping.

"Okay," Logan panted, looking like a terrified animal. "That was a little freaky."

Michael nodded emphatically. "Lafe thinks it was

58

'just a storm,'" he said, doing a perfect imitation of the senior's laid-back way of talking.

Quinn glanced around the room and suddenly realized something. "Hey, where are Zoey and Chase?" she asked worriedly.

Outside, an exhausted Chase set Zoey down on a PCA driveway curb as gently as he could.

"Okay, okay . . ." He tried not to sound as wiped out as he felt. Carrying a girl down a mountain was seriously exhausting by itself. Doing it while you were being chased by some kind of supernatural green fog was something else. He eyed the hills below Red Stone Gulch tenuously. "I think we're safe," he said, not sure if he was trying to convince himself or Zoey. "How're you?"

Zoey gingerly touched her sore ankle and tried to sort out the last hour in her head. It wasn't easy. "What happened up there?" she asked, searching Chase's face. Maybe he had some logical answers.

"A tornado?" Logan tossed out to the crew gathered in the lounge. They were looking for a way to explain the weird green moaning "thing," too.

"Yeah," Michael agreed sarcastically. "Just your average green tornado. Now come on, let's all just quit pretending we don't know what that was, because we all know exactly what it was." He wasn't all that excited about it, but the sooner they just admitted they had seen a ghost, the sooner they could move on.

"A swarm of radioactive fireflies?" Lafe suggested with a chuckle.

Michael stared daggers. First the guy got them lost in the foothills and now he was making idiotic suggestions. Ignoring the truth wasn't going to make it go away! "No. It wasn't a tornado," he insisted, giving Logan a smack on the back of the head. "Or fireflies. It was a —"

"Don't say it!" Logan begged, closing his eyes. He knew what Michael was about to say, and it was too freaky to think about. *Waaay* too freaky.

But Michael was not going to be deterred. "Ghost," he finished.

Logan scrunched his eyes tighter and covered his ears with his hands. "La-la-la-la-la-la-la-la-la-la-la," he said, shutting out Michael's words.

"It was the ghost of Charles Galloway," Michael said again as Logan leaped to his feet and la-la-la-ed even louder.

Michael was determined to get Logan to face the facts . . . or the ghost. Wasn't he the one who was determined to prove that Charles Galloway had existed in the first place? It wasn't all that surprising that the legend-come-true had a ghost attached to it. "Logan, you know it was his ghost," Michael insisted, standing right in front of his friend. "Stop la-la-la-ing."

"Logan, get a grip!" Quinn shouted from the edge of the sofa.

But only Logan knew that he had brought the dog tags back to PCA, that he had been the one to truly disturb the ghost and incur his wrath, so he couldn't listen to what Michael was saying. He had to block it out. Ignoring his friends, he kept on la-la-ing at the top of his lungs.

Outside, Chase was pacing. It seemed pretty obvious, and yet he just couldn't wrap his head around the idea.

"You really think it was a ghost?" Zoey asked, looking up at him.

Chase looked a little shaken up. "I don't know," he admitted. "I just never believed in all that stuff."

"Me either," Zoey agreed, trying to ignore the throbbing pain in her ankle. She was really wishing they'd never gone up to Red Stone Gulch at all.

Chase shook his head. This was crazy! There was no such thing as ghosts. "There's gotta be some sort of explanation," he said.

Zoey agreed, but what? "A trick?" she asked tenuously.

Chase shook his head. "C'mon, even Logan, with all his money and access to movie stuff, couldn't create a huge thunder and lightning storm and that . . . that green cloud thing, whatever that was," he added with a shudder. "Anyway, it's over," he finished, looking to the hills one more time.

"Yeah," Zoey agreed, rubbing her ankle. It was really getting swollen. "Ouch," she murmured.

"I gotta get you to the health center, to get that ankle looked at," Chase said, kneeling down beside her.

Zoey nodded. A bed and some ice would be good.

"Arms around my neck," Chase said as he braced himself to pick her up. As much as he loved having Zoey Brooks in his arms, he was still wiped out from carrying her down the mountain. He couldn't help but grunt a little as he lifted her off the ground.

Zoey looked peeved. "Don't groan when you lift me," she protested, sounding more like a pampered princess than a wounded student.

"I'm not used to carrying humans around in my arms for long distances," Chase defended.

"Well, maybe you should go to a gym," Zoey teased.

Chase tried not to smile. "Oh, the sass," he mused.

CHAPTER 9

Haunting

At the health center, Nurse Kafader was watching TV and doing a Rubik's Cube puzzle when the phone rang.

"PCA Health Center," she greeted. "Oh, hey, baby. No, it's mostly empty tonight. There's just one kid in here." She looked over at Dilson, who was sitting on her bed wearing pinstriped pajamas and working on some kind of elaborate Q-Tip structure. Dilson waved and smiled sheepishly. Was it her fault her economics teacher was verbally abusive?

"She had some kind of mental breakdown in class so the school psychologist put her in here for mental rest." She burst out in a menacing laugh.

"It's not funny," Dilson protested.

"Quiet, Crazy!" Nurse Kafader rapped out the order like a drill sergeant.

A horrified squeak was Dilson's only response.

Just then Chase and Zoey came through the door. "We're almost there," Chase encouraged. Zoey was walking now, but limping badly even with Chase supporting most of her weight. "Easy does it." Zoey leaned on him heavily. He led her into the room and looked over at the nurse.

"Hey, listen, I got a girl with a broken ankle here, I think," he said.

"Aw, crud," Nurse Kafader griped. "I'll call you later," she said into the phone before hanging up. "Put her on that bed over there," she told Chase.

"Right," Chase agreed, secretly relieved that they were finally at the health center. He knew Zoey's ankle hurt, but she was getting very cranky, and he was anxious for someone else to take care of her. Gingerly he eased her onto the bed.

"Ohhh, ow," Zoey said, wincing. Her ankle was really hurting. After sliding onto the bed and stretching out her legs, she carefully removed her backpack.

Chase reached toward her feet to take off one of her shoes.

"Don't touch it!" Zoey snapped.

Chase backed up against the wall. "I'm stupid," he admitted, holding up his hands in surrender.

"Zoey, what happened?" Dilson lisped, looking wide-eyed and sympathetic. "Some kind of accident?"

Zoey shot Chase a look. "Yeah, sorta."

"I see," Dilson said, nearly whistling through her retainer.

"Hey, can I use the phone?" Chase asked Nurse Kafader, a little reluctantly. She wasn't exactly the kind of person you wanted to mess with. PCA had not had the best luck with their health staff. Or at least Chase hadn't.

Nurse Kafader turned away from the cabinet of medical supplies. "I don't care," she said, giving Chase a sarcastic look.

Dropping Zoey's backpack at the foot of her bed, Chase picked up the phone. His friends were probably wondering if he and Zoey had been swallowed by the green fog. He had to let them know they were okay — and why they hadn't made it to the meeting point. Luckily he knew the number for the lounge by heart.

"Zoey, look!" Dilson said excitedly. She held up her carefully created structure proudly. "It's a Stonehenge menhir, made only of cotton swabs and white glue."

Zoey eyed Dilson and her structure, which had

obviously taken her hours to make. She knew she should say something nice about it, but just couldn't bring herself to do it. The squeaky girl and her swabs were almost as weird as the freaky green fog that had chased them down the mountain.

Michael heard the phone ring in the lounge and lurched toward it. "Lounge," he panted into the receiver. It was Chase! "Where are you? Okay, oohhh. Yeah, I'll be right there!"

By the time Michael hung up, everyone was on the edge of their seats.

"Chase?" Quinn asked, her brown eyes worried behind her square-framed glasses.

"Where are they?" Logan asked, stopping his la-la-las at last and getting out of his chair. This was something he *did* want to hear.

"The health center," Michael replied. "He thinks Zoey's got a broken ankle."

Lola was on her feet right away. "Oh, my God, I've gotta go," she said, moving toward the door, anxious to be by her friend's side.

"Okay," Lafe agreed as he got to his feet. "Oh, hey!" he called after Lola's retreating back.

Lola whirled around, her long dark hair flying around her shoulders.

"Um, I'm sorry I got you lost," Lafe apologized nervously.

Lola smiled up into Lafe's face. "Lost just means I found something I wasn't looking for," she said, forgiving him for everything.

"Wow." Lafe was bowled over. "It sounds so much less stupid when you say it."

"I know," Lola agreed. After all, she was an actress. She knew how to make every line sound fabulous!

Meanwhile, in the health center, Nurse Kafader was almost finished bandaging Zoey's ankle. "There," she said with satisfaction as she turned to pick up a tray. "Now, keep that leg still, eat that soup, and don't spit on the floor."

Zoey gave the nurse a look — did she look like a spitter? — but gratefully took the soup. She was starved!

"Aw, she can't spit on the floor?" Chase complained in a mocking voice. What kind of a rule was that? Did the nurse think they were in some sort of Wild West saloon?

"I don't like your brand of humor," Nurse Kafader said flatly, glaring at Chase as she slipped a pen into her pocket.

"Understood," Chase agreed, taking a seat on the stool next to Zoey's bed. He had no intention of getting on Nurse Kafader's bad side.

"I'm gonna go nuke a burrito," Nurse Kafader said, wiggling her fingers in the air excitedly as she headed out of the room. She was obviously a Mexican food fan.

Relieved that the nurse was gone, Chase pulled the stool a little closer to Zoey's bed. "So, things were pretty weird out there tonight," he began. He was having a hard time shaking off the creepy feeling in his gut.

"It couldn't have been a ghost," Zoey said, feeling a lot safer inside the health center walls. "Could it?" Her doubts and superstitions still nagged at her.

"If it was, it was definitely an angry ghost," Chase said, trying to ignore the vision of the slithering fog that kept popping into his head.

"I know," Zoey agreed. But she didn't really understand it. "Why?"

"Maybe Charles Galloway didn't like us messing

around his place . . . you know, I mean . . . the place where he used to live before he, uh . . . stopped living," Chase said, taking a guess.

"Oh, maybe it was just some kind of freaky weather thing," Zoey suggested, even though she knew in her heart that it was definitely not a freaky weather thing.

"Yeah, we'll just go with that," Chase said. They'd probably never know, and he was getting tired of talking about it. He'd rather just put it behind them. "Eat your soup."

Zoey picked up her spoon and looked into the bowl on the tray in her lap. But it wasn't soup . . . it was a bowl of slimy, disgusting, writhing worms! "Chase!" Zoey shrieked frantically.

"What?" Chase asked, hoping it wasn't anything too weird. Zoey's face said it all. She was terrified.

"Look in the bowl!" Zoey demanded. Why was he just sitting there? Couldn't he hear the slithering sound — or at least the panic in her voice?

Chase stood up and peered into the bowl. His heart stopped hammering. "Wow," he said casually. "You must really hate chicken noodle soup."

"Chicken noo —" Zoey braced herself for a second

look and peered into the bowl. Sure enough, it was just a bunch of yummy-looking noodles, chicken, and broth.

"You okay?" Chase asked. He was beginning to worry that their trip to Red Stone Gulch had messed up more than Zoey's ankle. Maybe she'd hit her head when she fell, too.

"Yeah," Zoey said, still eyeing the soup. "I guess I'm just . . . I'm just tired. Hiking all the way up to Red Stone Gulch just made me . . ."

Just then the nurse came back into the room carrying her burrito on a plate. She was just about to sit down at the reception desk when something fell to the floor. "Ugh, fork," she muttered as she bent down to pick it up.

While she was bending over, her back to Chase and Zoey, a ghostly green image of a face appeared on her rear end and laughed menacingly.

Zoey stared at it like she was in a trance. "Butt . . . face!" she stammered, pointing.

Nurse Kafader picked up her fork and whirled around. "What did you say?" she asked accusingly.

"Nothing . . . it's just . . . !" Zoey stammered again. How could she explain that she'd just seen an eerie face on the nurse's backside?

The nurse glared, obviously not convinced. Annoyed, she looked into her bag and got even more irritated. "I forgot the tomatillo salsa," she griped. "Watch the phones till I get back," she ordered, pointing at Chase.

As soon as she was out of the room, Zoey turned to Chase. She needed some serious reassurance. "You didn't see anything wrong, did you?" she quizzed worriedly. Maybe she was just losing it. Maybe she was going to spend the rest of her days making swab sculptures with Dilson!

"Well, I mean, sure." Chase shrugged. To be honest, he had been trying *not* to look, but since Zoey asked . . . "It wouldn't kill her to do some squats, you know, just to —"

"That's not what I meant!" Zoey protested.

"Maybe you just need some sleep," Chase suggested gently. He was more than a little worried. His best friend was clearly losing it!

"Yeah," Zoey agreed. She was exhausted. But then she remembered. . . . "Wait, I can't sleep! We have our economics test first thing in the morning," she reminded him. They had studying to do.

Outside, a low droning sound echoed in the air.

Lightning flashed. A strange green fog snaked across campus and under the health center door. A moment later, it was slithering around Zoey's backpack and the room was filled with a powerful wind. Papers and bandages flew everywhere!

"Uh...any idea what's going on here?" Zoey asked, looking around, frightened. Chase had to be seeing this, didn't he?

"No, not really!" Chase replied as the door slammed shut with a loud *BOOM* and locked by itself! He saw but he could not explain what was going on. The wind kept getting stronger and stronger and the arms on the clock started to spin uncontrollably.

Dilson was out of bed, struggling to find another way out. "Come open the window!" she called to Chase. But before he could even move, the cotton swab structure was lifted into the air and smashed against a wall.

"Ahhh, my swabs!" Dilson wailed miserably.

Who cares about cotton swabs? Chase wondered as a metal bucket lifted off the ground and moved toward Zoey. A second later, it slammed down on the top of her head.

"Ahhhh!" Zoey's screams echoed in the tin bucket.

"Zoey!" Chase shouted, crossing the room to her bed. He grabbed the bucket and tried to pull it off, but it wouldn't budge.

"Get this bucket off my head!" she shouted over the wailing wind.

"Aaaahhhhhh!" Dilson screamed again as a mass of green fog oozed in through the window and made its way across her bed.

Out on the pathway, Logan, Quinn, Michael, and Lola were hurrying to the health center.

"Will you guys slow down?" Logan complained. His legs ached from the hike to Red Stone Gulch. "It's just an injury."

"Be quiet," Lola snapped. "What did Chase say?" she quizzed Michael.

"That Zoey broke her ankle."

"How'd she break it?" Quinn asked.

"He didn't say!" Michael was just as frustrated as they were . . . and if they could all stop talking, they'd get to the health center a lot faster! "He just said that they were in the —"

Michael broke off and stared at the health center in the distance. The horrible green fog had followed them down the mountain and was now billowing out of the ceiling like smoke from a burning building. He could hear things crashing to the ground and the sound of someone screaming. Several someones.

"Aaaahhhhhh!" came a yell.

"Chaaaaasssseeee!" That was Zoey!

"Zoey!!!" a third, terrified voice called out.

"Ahhhhhh!"

The foursome stopped dead in their tracks and stared up at the health center windows.

"Okay." Logan tried to keep his voice steady. "That's not normal."

"N-nope," Quinn stuttered, shaking her head and wishing she could turn away. In all her years of scientific research, she had never seen — or heard — anything like this.

Lightning flashed right over the health center and the green fog moaned loudly. The screams coming from inside were completely garbled.

Michael stared in disbelief. One part of him wanted to go in there to help his friends. Another part wanted to run far, far away. But all of him just stood there like he was glued in place!

"Ahhhh!" Quinn and Lola screamed together.

Logan put his hands over his ears and closed his eyes. He had to block out as much of this as possible.

"La-la-la-la-la-la-la-la-la-la-la-la," he said over and over as loudly as he could.

There was no question about it. That green fog was the ghost of Charles Galloway. It was furious. It was after Chase and Zoey. And it was up to the others to rescue them.

CHAPTER 10

Green Fury

Inside the infirmary, the moaning green fog slithered across the floor, twisting around and around the beds, while papers, cotton swabs, and bits of debris whirled randomly in the air.

"Will somebody get this freakish bucket off my head?" Zoey yelled from inside her accidental helmet. She couldn't see a thing, and the moaning was getting louder and louder.

Chase banged on the locked door, twisting the handle in vain. "Why won't this door open?" he cried over the wind.

Suddenly Dilson's bed started to bounce up and down, bumping against the wall. "I want to go back to Massachusetts," Dilson wailed, squeezing her eyes shut tight. Nothing like this ever happened in Massachusetts, she thought. California was way weirder than people said.

Chase yanked on the door again — maybe he could break the handle off and get them out. . . .

Out in the courtyard, Logan, Michael, Lola, and Quinn stared at the health center. It looked like some kind of possessed factory belching out toxic green smoke.

And then, while they stared, the green fog merged together into a kind of circle and a giant ghostly face appeared in the sky.

"Waaah-ahh-ahh-ahh!" the face laughed menacingly.

"It's the ghost of Charles Galloway!" Michael cried, pointing shakily at the apparition. He was big. He was ugly. And he was mad.

"No it's not!" Logan insisted, grabbing the arm of Lola's black T-shirt. "You tell him there's no such thing as ghosts," he begged.

Lola's eyes were as big as saucers and her long dark hair was whipping wildly around her face. "O-okay," she stammered. "I'll tell Michael, but you have to tell that ghost over there!"

"You guys!" Quinn shrieked. Everyone seemed to be forgetting an important detail. "Zoey and Chase are in there!"

Michael lurched forward. "We gotta go help them!" he shouted, moving toward the ghost and ignoring the voices in his head screaming for him to run.

"You help them," Logan advised, trying not to sound like a wimp.

Michael balked. "What, the three of you are just going to let me go in there alone?"

"Yes!" all three of them said at once. Lola even lifted a hand in a panicked good-bye wave.

Michael wanted to throttle each and every one of them but didn't have time. Giving them one last "I can't believe you" look, he headed toward the main entrance to the health center and, before he could change his mind, yanked open the door.

In the center's entrance hall, things looked pretty normal. If it weren't for the frantic screams coming from inside, Michael might have thought things were relatively sane.

Racing up to the door, Michael tried the handle, but it was locked. Michael pounded on the door. "Chase! Zoey! You in there?" he called.

"Michael, is that you?" Chase yelled through the door. It was practically impossible to hear over the wind.

Michael looked around worriedly. That creepy green ghost fog could come under the door and get him at any second! He could hear it howling on the other side. "Dude, I think something weird is going on in there!" Michael warned.

Chase stared at the door in disbelief. "Yah *think*?" he asked sarcastically.

"Who are you talking to?" Zoey asked from under her bucket. She felt abandoned and helpless in her dark metal prison and half wondered if Chase had started up a conversation with the ghost of Charles Galloway. She could barely hear and could not see a blasted thing!

"Michael," Chase yelled to Zoey. Turning back to the door he shouted, "Michael, you gotta get this door open!" The ghost of Charles Galloway was not chilling out and he did not want to be trapped with it one second longer!

"Okay, stand back. I'll break it down," Michael yelled.

"Okay," Chase agreed, backing away from the door. If anyone could break down a door, it was Michael. The dude was pretty big and in great shape.

Michael took several giant steps back to get a running start. Then, bracing himself, he ran toward the door.

Just as he approached, the lock clicked and the door swung wide open. But it was too late for Michael to stop his forceful run. He hurtled across the room and slammed — *thud!* — right into the wall. Ugh. Michael landed on the floor in a heap.

Furious and aching, Michael got to his feet. "Why did you open the door?" he accused, rubbing his shoulder through his sleeveless PCA sweatshirt.

Chase shrugged, his eyes wide. This was *waaaaay* too weird. He'd rather be studying for his economics test — or even taking it! "It opened by itself!" he said.

"Who are you talking to?" Zoey asked again, her voice echoing. Between the wind and the bucket, it was impossible to hear anything.

"Why does Zoey have a bucket over her head?" Michael yelled.

Just then Dilson's bed bucked and she rolled off the edge. Screaming, she scrambled to her shaky feet. "I'm so out of here!" she wailed, throwing her arms in the air and shrieking, running into the hall for the second time that day.

"We need to get out of this room," Michael yelled as Dilson disappeared.

Chase shook his head. "Zoey can't walk," he explained. As wigged out as he was, he wasn't going anywhere without her. And he didn't know if he could carry her another step.

"There's a gurney in the hall," Michael suggested.

"Help me get her!" Chase said. He grabbed Zoey's shoe from the floor and put it on her foot as gently as he could under the circumstances.

"Ow!" Zoey yelped from beneath her bucket.

Michael and Chase helped her to her feet. While Chase half carried her into the hall, Michael grabbed her backpack and kept an eye out for any incoming flying objects. He slammed the door to the health center, leaving the raging wind and green glowing fog behind him.

"Careful with me!" Zoey complained as they lurched together to the gurney. Her ankle was throbbing and she was starting to feel a little claustrophobic. "Just get this stupid bucket off my head!" she begged.

Chase gave the bucket a couple of yanks but it still didn't budge. "I can't!" he exclaimed, frustrated. "It's stuck . . . just hang on."

Behind them Michael saw the green fog begin to ooze out from underneath the door. They weren't in the clear yet — not by a long shot. "Go! Go! Go!" he bellowed.

Chase yanked on his end of the gurney, pulling it down the hallway. A few seconds later, they burst through the double doors into the night air.

Lola, Logan, and Quinn stared in astonishment.

"Are you guys okay?" Quinn asked, thrilled to see her friends but still freaked out and more than a little perplexed by the ghost.

"Not really!" Zoey said, pointing to the bucket that was, for all she knew, permanently attached to her head. She struggled to get it off, but it would not budge.

"What's happening?" Lola asked.

"I'm not sure," Chase said, letting go of the gurney and leaning over to gulp some air. "But I think that's the ghost of Charles Galloway."

"I'm sure!" Michael groaned. Why couldn't they just agree that they were being tortured by a ghost?

"What do we do?" Chase cried.

Out of the corner of his eye, Michael saw the gurney rolling down the sloped pathway — with Zoey still on it! "I think you should go get Zoey!" he yelled.

From inside the bucket, Zoey's voice sounded tinny. "What's happening?" she asked. Her friends' voices were fading. She felt movement. "Am I rolling?"

"Hold on!" Chase called out to her. "I'll be back!" he told his friends. "Figure out a way to get rid of that ghost!"

Zoey felt the wheels of the gurney go over some

bumps and pick up speed. Yep. She was definitely rolling. Blind. Trapped. Injured. And rolling. "I am gonna kill
somebody!" she threatened as she careened around a
corner.

"There's no such thing as ghosts!" Logan insisted.
He prayed his words were true. If they weren't, he was
in big trouble. As long as he could just keep denying the
existence of ghosts, then —

Whoosh! The health center doors flew open and a
giant mass of the swirling green fog bellowed into the
night with a force so strong that everyone was thrown
a step back.

"Ok-k-k-ay," Michael stuttered. "Either that's a
ghost, or the health center just sneezed."

Suddenly Quinn got an idea. "I know what to do!"
she said. "Come help me!"

She didn't have to ask twice. Logan, Lola, and
Michael took off after her. No matter what her idea was,
it was better than standing around waiting to be attacked
by an angry, undeniably real ghost.

Antidote

A few minutes later, Quinn, Michael, Lola, and Logan were gathered in Quinn's room. A suitcase of mysterious jars and containers was open on the end of her bed, and Quinn, seated at a small workspace, was telling her friends what to do.

"Hurry!" she cried as they handed her the materials she needed to make the ghost antidote.

"I am!" Logan groused as he opened a second case full of sciency stuff.

"We're hurrying!" Lola echoed.

"I got the site up," Michael said over his shoulder. He'd been busy surfing the Internet for information on ghosts. "Paranormal four-one-one dot com," he reported.

"Search for astromagnaplasm and read me

everything it says," Quinn directed as she slid on a pair of protective glasses.

"Astromagnaplasm," Michael said the word slowly as he typed it in.

"Hand me the cobalt jellicon," Quinn rattled off to Lola.

"The cobalt jello-what?" Lola asked, completely lost. There were, like, six jars in this case — she needed her instructions in English! "The blue jiggly stuff in that thing!" she said, pointing. This was not the time to get technical — a paranormal thingy was after them!

Lola grabbed a big jar of blue goop and handed it to the scientist. "Like I should know what jellicose means," she grumbled to herself.

Quinn took the jar and set it on the table next to her tiny bunson burner. This was taking forever! "Gimme that tub of crystallized actoparticles," she demanded.

Logan picked up a jar of light blue crystal-looking rocky stuff and set it on the table.

"Yes!" Quinn confirmed that it was the correct jar before lighting her tiny torch. Waiting to hear more from Michael, she heated a large crystallized actoparticle over the flame.

"Here, here we go," Michael said, reading from the screen. "Astromagnaplasm: the event of a noncorporeal manifestation of the spirit or soul of a person that has remained on earth after the person's passing . . ."

Outside, Chase was racing after Zoey and the gurney as it sped faster and faster down the PCA walkway.

"Zoey! Slow down!" he yelled, even though he knew that was a ridiculous request. She had no control over her speed — she couldn't even see, for cripes' sake! But Chase was exhausted and desperate. He had to reach her before she got to that long flight of —

"Stairs!" Chase shouted.

"What?" Zoey could barely hear him. In her helmet world, all she heard was the squeaking gurney wheels and her own ragged breathing.

"Stairs!" Chase shouted again.

"What stairs?" Zoey cried, suddenly filled with panic. She was going to roll down stairs?

Grabbing the edge of the bucket with both hands, she yanked with all her might and it came off! Zoey was momentarily thrilled to be able to see and to breathe normally. But what she saw made her want to block it all out again. Stairs!

"Jump! Now!" Chase shouted.

Zoey threw herself off the edge of the gurney onto the grass, doing her best not to land on her hurt ankle.

"Wow, you jumped," Chase panted, running up to where Zoey lay in the grass. He was impressed. Crouching down next to Zoey, he looked to make sure she was okay.

"Why didn't you get the bucket off my head?" Zoey demanded. She'd practically suffocated in there! "What is the matter with you!" She started hitting him on the legs — and didn't stop.

Yep. Zoey was okay! At least okay enough to give him a hard time. "Stop it!" he said, grabbing her hands. It had been the freakiest day he could remember, and he needed calm, rational Zoey back, pronto.

Taking a deep breath, Zoey tried to calm down. The bucket wasn't Chase's fault, of course. He'd tried to pull it off at least twice, and said it was stuck. She hadn't been able to get it off, either, so she knew he was telling the truth . . . even if believing that meant believing a ghost was in control.

She was about to let Chase off the hook when she heard a bloodcurdling scream come from the bottom of the stairs . . . just as the gurney disappeared over the top.

"Eeeeee!" A loud and familiar squeak echoed in the night air as a shower of cotton swabs flew skyward. Dilson. The gurney had landed — right on top of her.

Chase and Zoey exchanged a look. That had to hurt.

Below them, lying on the stairs with cotton swabs sticking out of her mouth, Dilson pondered her horrible luck. First Mr. Hodges insulted her terribly in class. Then the school nurse called her crazy. Some weird ghostly thing attacked her in the health center. And now a renegade gurney had run her down! It was all too much. "My life is an endless vortex of pain," she mumbled to herself. "Waaah, waaaah, waaah," she squeaked.

Half walking, half carrying Zoey, Chase made his way back to her dorm to help his friend get settled. They both needed some serious rest.

"Slow down!" Zoey complained, limping along as best she could. Her ankle was killing her, her clothes were rumpled, and she felt like a complete mess.

"Do you want that green whatever it is to catch us?" Chase asked pointedly, trying to hurry.

"No, but I have ankle issues," she reminded him grimly. Did he think she was limping for fun?

Just then Logan, Michael, Lola, and Quinn came running up behind them.

"Are you okay?" Lola asked.

Zoey shot her a look. "I've had better nights. You know, when my ankle didn't break and a ghost wasn't trying to kill us?" she said sarcastically. She knew none of that was actually Lola's fault, but she had reached her limit.

"Don't worry," Lola said, panting. Her friends were fast runners; she'd struggled to keep up and did not like to get sweaty. But it would all be worth it if they could really get rid of the ghost.

"Yeah, Quinn's got us hooked up." Michael handed Quinn the small camera bag he was holding and she pulled out a pair of glowing, almost-round balls.

"What are those? Are they gonna explode?" Zoey asked, nervously eyeing Quinn's latest inventions. It wasn't like her to be so negative, but she couldn't take any more problems tonight. And she could not run.

"No," Quinn promised, handing one to Michael. "Not right now."

"This jellicon orb contains positively charged ion particles, and this one," she added, pointing to the one Michael was holding, "contains negatively —"

"Human words, Quinn," Zoey said impatiently. She couldn't take any more of this nonsense! "Human words."

"When the ghost appears, I throw this orb at it," Quinn stated plainly.

"And I throw this one," Michael added.

"And they'll rupture, each releasing a gaseous burst of kinetic bioenergy —"

"Quinn!" Zoey snapped in exasperation. What part of *human words* didn't the girl understand?

"It'll make the ghost go away," Quinn finished. "There, did you understand that?"

"Let's just do this!" Logan interrupted. If that whatever it was showed up again, he was going to have to get back to his la-la-las!

"Okay, but how do we attract the ghost?" Lola wanted to know.

Michael's eyes widened. "I don't think that's gonna be too tough," he said. There was a note of terror in his voice.

Everyone turned and saw the green fog snake its way around the corner of a brick building.

"And . . . here he comes," Chase stammered. He seriously hoped that Quinn's orbs worked on the ghost as well as her snake deterrent had worked on the cactus earlier. Otherwise it looked as though they'd be haunted by the ghost of Charles Galloway forever!

"I'm ready to throw my gaseous orb!" Michael said, shaking so badly he nearly dropped it.

"no!" Quinn said, steadying his arm. "We can't do it outside; we have to do it in a sealed environment."

"What?" Michael asked in a frantic whisper.

Ugh. What was wrong with these people? Didn't they understand anything? "A room!" Quinn explained impatiently. They had to throw the orbs in a room.

"Come on, let's go," Chase said, bracing himself to take the weight off of Zoey's ankle.

The six students hurried inside the closest building. "Ow, ow, ow, ow, ow," Zoey yelped at each step on the way into their economics classroom. Even with Chase helping her, every bump made her ankle ache.

"Okay, everyone against the wall," Quinn instructed in a whisper.

Everyone obediently backed up against the far wall of the classroom and stood in a huddle.

"now what?" Michael asked anxiously.

"When it comes through the door, I'll yell 'orbs away,' and then we throw them right at its center," Quinn instructed.

"I'm gonna lose an eye," Chase whimpered pathetically. "I just know I'm gonna lose an eye!"

"Shhh!" Logan hissed.

"Just watch the door!" Lola added, pressing her back to the window behind her.

Michael held the orb in the air, ready to fire . . . and then felt something snake its way around his legs. Looking down, he saw the green fog enveloping his lower half.

"I-I-I-I-I," he stammered, too scared to speak. "I don't think it's coming through the door!" he finally managed to squeak out as the fog slithered around everyone's legs.

"Get away from the window!" Quinn instructed.

Screaming, they all raced away from the window to the other side of the room just as a larger mass of fog slipped into the room.

"Quinn, will you say 'orbs away' already?" Zoey shrieked.

"Are you ready, Michael?"

Michael's eyes were wide with fear, and he looked completely frozen.

"Ready?" Quinn repeated. "Ready?" There was no response.

"Just gimme it," Zoey said, reaching over and grabbing the orb from Michael. There was no time to panic!

"Orbs away!" Quinn shouted, and she and Zoey threw the balls directly into the mass of fog.

Colored bolts of lightning flashed, and the green fog moaned wildly as a dark smoke filled the air. There was a loud explosion and everyone was thrown to the floor. By the time the lightning stopped and everyone opened their eyes, the classroom was practically destroyed. The window blinds were bent or missing altogether, the desks were flipped over, and several chairs were broken. A thick smoke hung in the air. And it didn't smell exactly fresh.

"I think it worked," Michael said, squinting through the smoke.

"Yeah," Lola agreed. "It's gone."

Quinn smiled with satisfaction. Take that, Charles Galloway!

But before anyone made a move to leave the classroom, a familiar green fog slithered in beneath the windows. Chase gulped. "Well, hello again," he said, a massive lump in his gut.

The swirl of green grew.

"Okay, Quinn," Zoey said, staring at the fog and

half wishing she had that bucket on her head again. "Now what?"

"Well, speaking scientifically..." Quinn screeched. There was only one answer to that question. "Run!"

Nobody had to be convinced. They leaped over fallen tables and broken chairs, racing for the door.

Outside, lightning flashed and wind gusted. Charles Galloway was definitely still with them. The group raced to a concealed corner between buildings and crouched together in a huddle.

"Why does the ghost of Charles Galloway hate us?" Michael asked. They'd tried to destroy it and it had come back. But if they could figure out what it wanted...

"And keep attacking us?" Zoey added.

"I guess he's mad because we disturbed his eternal resting place," Quinn suggested. It was the only thing that made sense.

"But we left things just like we found them," Chase whined.

"Yeah, we put his dog tags back and everything," Zoey agreed.

Out of the corner of her eye, Zoey saw Logan

flinch. "You put the necklace back . . . didn't you?" she asked accusingly. "Didn't you?"

Logan didn't answer.

"Didn't you?" Michael was about ready to pummel him.

It was time to face the music, Logan realized. It had to be better than facing a ghost. "Hand me your backpack," he told Zoey grimly.

Zoey shot Chase a "this does not sound good" look and handed him her backpack. Taking it, Logan unzipped one of the small outside compartments and pulled out Charles Galloway's necklace.

A chorus of angry "no ways" erupted from everyone.

"Are you kidding me?" Michael cried. He looked like he was about to explode. "I can't believe you, Logan."

"We gotta put that necklace back," Chase insisted.

"I say we beat the snot out of Logan first," Michael said. It was taking some serious restraint not to pound him right now.

"No!" Zoey shouted over the din.

"No?" Michael couldn't believe it. Wasn't Zoey the one Charles Galloway had been after all night?

"We put back the necklace, then we beat the snot

out of Logan," she stated, shooting him a murderous glare.

Everyone was talking at once as they got to their feet. "I have issues with this plan," Logan protested feebly.

"If that ghost doesn't kill you, I will!" Michael vowed.

CHAPTER 12

Back Where It Belongs

By early morning everyone was standing around Charles Galloway's resting place. Logan silently dropped the necklace into a shallow hole in the dirt and they all covered it up with their hands, patting the soil into place.

Chase had never been so glad to get rid of something in his life — and he hadn't even known they had the necklace in the first place! "So, uh, should we say some words?" he asked, looking over at Zoey.

Zoey nodded and quickly tried to come up with something to say. Given the horrible night she'd had, and the painful climb to get back to Charles's grave on her twisted ankle, her first thought was to ask Charles's ghost to torture Logan for the rest of his days, but she wasn't that cruel. "Well, Charles . . ." she began. "We're sorry we disturbed you. We're sorry we took your necklace . . . but it's back now, so please stop terrifying us?" Zoey finished her little speech in a questioning voice, in case somebody else wanted to say something. And because it was really weird to be standing there talking to a ghost!

"Amen!" everyone else said together, glad to be done.

A long thin band of green fog zoomed past them and disappeared into the ground in the exact same spot as Charles's necklace.

Nobody was surprised; everyone was relieved.

"There, it's done," Quinn said, feeling like a giant burden had been lifted off their shoulders.

"Good," Logan said, though he couldn't shake the anxious feeling he was having. The ghost might be satisfied, but Michael could come after him at any moment!

Fortunately for Logan, Michael was too tired to follow through on his threats. "I can't believe we've been up all night," he complained, looking up at the rocky canyon that surrounded them.

Zoey glanced down at her watch. What time was it, anyway? . . . "Our econ exam!" she blurted. It started in less than an hour!

"And we get a zero if we're late!" Michael remembered aloud.

"So run!" Quinn advised, once again relieved that she hadn't signed up for that horrible class.

Logan, Michael, and Chase took off at a breakneck pace.

"I can't run, I have a broken ankle!" Zoey reminded them.

Michael turned on his heel and raced back to Zoey. "Come on, jump on, Brooks," he said.

Zoey obediently hopped onto Michael's back and he took off running, then turned back to Lola and Quinn. "Say good luck," he told them.

"Good luck!" the girls chorused.

With a nod, Michael turned back around and headed after Logan and Chase. They would need all the luck they could get if they were going to get to class in time.

Back at PCA, Mr. Hodges was in an uproar. "I want to know who did this!" he bellowed at the class, who sat obediently in chairs that had no desks, surrounded by broken window blinds, papers, and other debris.

"What did you think," he continued, "that by

vandalizing my classroom you would get out of taking this exam?" He waved the stack of papers he held in his hand angrily. "Who did this to my classroom?" he roared.

Just then Zoey, Logan, Chase, and Michael tumbled through the door in a virtual heap.

"Hello," Zoey said tentatively.

"Hi," Chase panted.

"We're here." Michael had to lean over to catch his breath.

"You're late!" Mr. Hodges roared.

"We know," Zoey admitted as Chase helped her into a chair. It felt incredibly good to sit down.

"Yeah," Chase agreed. For some strange reason he felt compelled to tell everyone what had happened to the classroom. "This is going to sound really weird, but last night . . . our friend Quinn, she had these two glowing balls of —"

"Just sit down!" Mr. Hodges ordered. "I am trying to find out which one of these hooligans destroyed this classroom!"

Michael couldn't help but laugh. After spending the night being chased by the ghost of Charles Galloway, Mr. Hodges seemed like a kitten. "Oh, uh, that was kind of us," he said, gesturing to himself and his friends.

"You!" Mr. Hodges looked ready to charge.

"Well, I mean, it wasn't our fault, exactly," Chase insisted.

"Yeah," Zoey chimed in a little hesitantly. "Actually, it was the ghost of Charles Galloway."

"What?" Mr. Hodges looked even angrier now. His face turned a darker shade of purple and the veins on his neck bulged. "Is this some sort of joke?" he demanded.

"No," Michael stammered. "He was your student," Michael pointed out, trying to sound rational.

"Fifty years ago," Logan confirmed.

"And you know how the legend goes that he supposedly went up to Red Stone Gulch —"

"Silence!" Mr. Hodges roared. "I've heard that silly legend for half a century, and it *is* a lie!"

"Yeah, not really," Zoey said warningly.

"Charles Galloway never went up to Red Stone Gulch, and there's no such thing as ghosts!" Mr. Hodges insisted.

Miles away, someone else was listening, and a band of green fog shot out of the ground and raced down the mountain. Within seconds, it was heading across campus.

"What was that?" a PCA student asked as the flash of green passed by.

In his demolished classroom, the economics teacher was still on a rant. "...Since you children have such active imaginations, perhaps I should give you all —"

The band of green swept into the room and wrapped itself around the aging teacher, interrupting him and spinning him in a dizzying circle.

"Whoooaaaaaa!" Mr. Hodges screamed while the ghost of Charles Galloway laughed menacingly.

Then, as quickly as it had appeared, the snaky green fog darted out the door and disappeared, leaving Mr. Hodges standing in the middle of the room looking a little like he'd been struck by lightning. His glasses were askew and his clothes were rumpled. More than that, his brain was scrambled.

Everyone gaped at the teacher and waited for him to speak.

"Your exam is canceled," he finally managed to mutter before he walked shakily out of the room. "Class dismissed!"

Everyone cheered, and Logan, Chase, and Michael high-fived ecstatically. Even Dilson was happily beaming over the top of her new neck brace.

Zoey looked up at the hills, exhausted and grateful. "Thanks, Charles," she said as the green fog rapidly disappeared into the ground yet again — this time, forever.